DARK
TRANSFORMATIONS:

DEADLY VISIONS
OF CHANGE

MICHAEL R. COLLINGS

BORGO PRESS / WILDSIDE PRESS

www.wildsidepress.com

Library of Congress Cataloging-in-Publication Data

Collings, Michael R.
  Dark Transformations : deadly visions of change / Michael R. Collings
    p. cm.
  ISBN 1-55742-197-8 : $16.95 – ISBN 1-55742-196-X (pbk.) : $8.95
  1. Fantastic literature, American 2. Change – Literary collections.
  I. Title.
  PS3553.0474696D3 1989
    811'.54 – dc20   89-26101
                                                                          CIP

Earlier versions of these poems appeared as: "Bodies," in *Dialogue: A Journal of Mormon Thought*; "Colony," in *In Memoriam: A Father...and a Friend*; "Gargoyles," in *The Leading Edge*; "On the First Outdoor Testing...," in *1988 Odyssey Awards*; "The SoulOrgan," "Star Pilot's Funeral," and "The Star Scout Handbook," in *Star*Line*; "Succubi," in *Footsteps VIII*; "When the Wordmonger Came," in *The Leading Edge*; "Wiros," in *Naked to the Sun: Dark Visions of Apocalypse* (1985), "A Midnight Horror Reading at the Stanley Hotel," in *Horrorfest Press*, "Crucifax (for Ray Garton)," "Our Gods Have Died," and "Faces of Fear (for Dean R. Koontz)," in The Blood Review: The Journal of Horror Criticism

DR. MICHAEL R. COLLINGS is Professor of English and Director of Creative Writing at Pepperdine University. His publications range from poetry (including *A Season of Calm Weather* and *Naked to the Sun*), to book-length critical studies of the works of Piers Anthony, Brian W. Aldiss, Stephen King, and Orson Scott Card. His books for Starmont House include: *Piers Anthony* (1983); *Stephen King as Richard Bachman* (1985); *The Shorter Works of Stephen King*, with David A. Engebretson (1985); *The Many Facets of Stephen King* (1985); *Naked to the Sun: Dark Visions of Apocalypse* (1985); *Brian W. Aldiss* (1986); *The Films of Stephen King* (1986); *The Annotated Guide to Stephen King* (1986); and *The Stephen King Phenomenon* (1987).

As always—

For Judith, *F.T.A.A.E*

DARK
TRANSFORMATIONS:
Deadly Visions
of Change

CONTENTS

Part One:
The Way of the Wolf

Dark Transformations

Light and Night transform warm blood,
Each to its own blueprint flesh and bone.

Light's slender shivering touch
Burns blood, elevates beyond weight's harsh reach,
Completes with liquid flesh the body's ink-wash sketch.

But Night...evil Night confirms
The stone-slash heart, the ice-pick point of vermin
Fangs, the gallows-eyes that slay and tear and burn.

Night's fingers numbly slip
Through crevices of change to shatter what hides deep,
Rend black blocks that bridge abysmal gaps

And from their crippled wreck
Conflate yet darker forms in blood-pain wracked
That crush stained flesh on adamantine rock.

And so, to its own blueprint flesh and bone,
Black Night and Light each vessels of blood transform.

Wiros

Here shadowed from the seeing, seering sun
this body seems me/mine almost—
or I its. I do not know.

I run. The blade in my heart matches the blade
in my hand. Blood streams naked thighs
flashing red as I run—

hot red from my kill, terrifying yet perversely attracting.
Within cool shadows quarry-eyes
cower. They know I *am*,

but not who or what. They fear the phantom-shadow
that swoops by day to kill
and kill.

By night they search but will not, cannot find,
cannot know I walk among them
as they search, am

the beast—and in darkness I will not know either.
But now I run, naked in sunset, bleeding from
briars, heart

hammered by the demon I am become—hideous body erect,
hairless, clawless, fangless, slaying brothers. I weep
to die and cannot.

Day-nightmare, by night oblivion of reality.   For with
black night, I will transform into
          the wolf again

Wer Means Man

He woke to pain and fear and confusion.

His last Memory was of a place without a scent, a mountain that whispered of strangeness and danger.

He had trekked unfamiliar territory for three days, farther from the Boundaries than he had ever ranged. The air had grown steadily thinner, drier, oppressively drier even at dark, in spite of bitter waters that sometimes oozed over smooth stones and crossed flatlands dotted with hillocks of harsh grasses.

He raised his head and looked around.

He had done the unthinkable. He had transgressed the Boundaries, but there had been no choice. The cry had called to him in his sleep after the last hunt, had driven him from the pack, had haunted him from range to range. Even now, he could sense it faintly ahead.

He began to walk. Slowly, laboriously. His panting spoke not only of fatigue nearing exhaustion but also of high altitudes and fugitive air.

He approached a treeless pass bordered by cliffs that soared into clouds hanging thick and grey.

He stopped. Sniffed.

The hackles on his neck rose. A growl welled from deep in his throat. His fangs glistened in the dim light.

Wrongness throbbed beyond a bush whose naked branches cracked like brittle bones in the wind.

He listened, cocking his ears right, left.

There were no sounds of small scurryings in dry grasses. His breath rasped loudly.

For the first time, he felt fear. Beneath his thick pelt, his skin quivered. He dropped his muzzle, whining like a day-old pup.

And then....something squeezed against his brain, behind his eyes, a pressure that swelled like a pack of packs to seethe in hatred and fear and shift to something new, a cry unlike the echoes he had followed.

He fought against fear and steadied himself to leap. His nose lifted to test the air.

There! The prey flickered, thin, elongated white flash lit by the rising Small Bright that scuttled low beneath the fringed clouds. Something tall, hideous, just downwind. As he swiveled toward it, the thing disappeared.

In spite of the throbbing pressure behind his eyes, he moved. He concentrated on the scent, on stealth, on the kill. He became the shadow of a shadow, silent and lethal.

He crept forward. And leaped.

The cry sounded again—then there was a sudden crash of thunder-louder-than-thunder in his ears and fire blossomed through his shoulder.

He spun like lightning, twisting against the flame that spread from his shoulder throughout his body. Beyond his vision, something rushed toward him. He felt the jarring shock of bone against bone. His teeth grasped, ripped. His mouth filled suddenly with a viscous warmth that nauseated and thrilled. The strange cry rose again, twisted with fear and with pain that rocked his mind as the pressure exploded and everything went frighteningly black.

He fell forward against a granite shard that struck his injured shoulder. He spun sideways, and a dead branch caught him under the jaw and flipped him over.

He was already unconscious when he landed in the thornbush.

* * * * *

He woke to pain and fear and confusion. Without opening his eyes, he sniffed.

His head jerked up.

He was in his own den! He tried to stretch, but winced, then whined in sudden pain. His shoulder burned.

He struggled up, shook himself carefully.

She crouched nearby, eyes staring steadily at him, muzzle resting against the hard-packed earth.

He licked the matted blood on his shoulder and looked back at her.

She seemed satisfied. She loped out of the den, returning almost immediately to drop something in front of him.

It was freshly dead, large and plump. He tore at the warm flesh and swallowed it. It removed the last haunting echoes of the bad taste at the same time it killed the throbbing pain in his gut.

Then he slept.

Two lights later he limped out to the sun-stone. He lay quietly, muzzle on forepaws. He was worried. His Memory—the Memory he and the pack would depend on to find hunting trails in the darkness of snow-time—seemed damaged. He could see everything during his trek, everything up to the moment of the thunder-that-was-not-thunder and the burning in his shoulder, but nothing after that. Until he roused in his own den, there was only a frightening blank. If he should forget other things—the trail to the low grounds, the place of water beneath the high rocks—he and the pack might die.

He closed his eyes. The sun beat down on his spine. There was little pain in his shoulder now, only an occasional stiffness and a swelling just above the bone.

* * * * *

He healed. Matted fur closed over the wound, new tissue grew, pain died. He was well except for a small, hard lump near his shoulder, an occasional grating of bone against tender flesh, and an insistent warmth that sometimes spidered out from the lump. He was all right.

But he was troubled. The blanks in his Memory still disturbed him, although less now. There were no new blanks. And he had no trouble remembering during the hunts, following the trails as he had before he traveled into the beyond place.

Twice he hunted with her, away from the pack, testing his skills. They were intact. As soon as he could run without any twitches from the wound, he would resume leadership. Snow-time was many lights away—the air smelled of coolness but not of biting cold. And until then, the darks were wonderful for hunting, as he and she crept among the greenery, sharing warm flesh and hot blood. More than once they lingered in the forests until long after light, spending their energy in mock-battles that merged unnoticed with mating.

* * * * *

He was dozing when the scream shattered the air, startling him from disturbing sleep-shadows. His head jerked up as the scream died.

Then the keening rose.

He leaped...and nearly fell when his shoulder buckled under him. The wound was painful again, agonizingly stiff. He limped to the sun-stone and picked his way down the trail and across the meadow toward yearlings and cubs clustered at the edge of the forest.

The scream ripped the air again. Fear and agony and anger twined through the long, harsh cadences. He trembled. He forced himself forward in spite of cutting pain. He bit at his shoulder, as if checking for blood. There was none—only the heady musk of himself and a lingering trace of her and...and a strange, heavy odor that tingled his nostrils and almost made him stumble.

But the keening rose again and the errant scent fled as he nipped his way through clustered yearlings, snapping viciously when one blundered against his shoulder.

Then he stopped.

An old one lay dead.

The muzzle was spotted with foam, the eyes distended as if the old one were still struggling for breath. But the old one was dead.

He looked up, following the trail of ripped branches and torn moss where the old one had fallen down the slope, as if out of a need to die within scent of the pack. The air held an acrid scent, unknown yet hauntingly familiar.

Someone growled. He looked up in time to see her enter the circle. Their eyes met. She backed away, whirled, and ran.

Her cry had awakened him.

By now, other adults were emerging from the trees. He nuzzled the corpse once more. There were bruises, and the old one's pelt was matted with twigs and grass and dirt—but there was no wound that could kill. The only blood was already crusting around a small hole in the old one's forehead.

But such a small wound surely could not kill!

He looked up.

Three yearlings broke from the circle and stepped around him and tugged at the old one's stiffening legs, pulling the body from the pack's grounds.

He watched the body disappear. He felt weak. His shoulder burned as he limped back to the den, crossing the sun-stone without even thinking once of laying full-length in the warmth and sleeping. Instead, he disappeared into the dark shadows of the den and the waiting coolness.

During the next three lights, three more old ones died. All were light-hunting, even though they might have hunted by dark just as easily. Each had slipped through early mists for private hunting grounds.

All were found with small wounds in their heads and the lingering scent of something acrid and hot surrounding them. He went with the others to see the first one. After that, he refused.

17

He also refused to eat. And now she was acting strangely as well. She avoided him, bristling when he touched her, so he nipped back in frustration and growled throatily when she entered the den, or snapped when she came too near. On the third light-end since the first old one died, he woke to an empty den. She did not return that dark, or the next.

During the fourth dark after the coming of Death to the pack, he did not sleep. He lay motionless for what seemed a lifetime of breaths. He hurt with a deep, burning pain that was more than pain, that slipped through his body like a fog. When he tried to catch it, to bite and worry it and finally to kill it, he could not find it. Instead, he twisted and whined and twitched with irritation of the pain-not-pain.

Finally he rose and padded from the den, gliding away into shadows. He saw no one, even though the Small Bright had risen. Clouds covered most of the sky. He threaded through dense undergrowth, pausing once when he thought he heard the faint crackling of steps behind him. He swiveled his head, eyes and ears straining for sounds or movement.

There was nothing.

He continued, weaving through underbrush as silently as a shadow, following a Memory that he could not see, a new Memory that terrified as much as it enticed.

As he went, he felt no fear of the Death that stalked the pack. In fact, he moved with increasing confidence, increasing strength as the pain-not-pain receded and his muscles warmed.

He stopped at the base of a towering black cliff. Again, he had the prickling feeling that someone...*something*...was trailing him in the darkness. He glared over his shoulder, snarling a challenge. Dark swallowed the sound. After a few breaths, he began climbing the rocks, following a faint trail through coarse gravel and littered leaves.

The climb was difficult. His paws slipped on the rocks, once slamming him against the cliff face. But he continued until he reached a ledge mid-way up the cliff face.

From there, he could see the entire valley. He settled his body into a hollow littered with small stones and dead leaves, rested his muzzle on his forepaws, and waited.

None of the pack was ranging during this dark. No movement disturbed the world below him.

He waited. Finally he slept.

But this sleep brought no rest. His fevered mind whirled so rapidly that the Memory clicked in, engraving sleep-shadows onto his brain. It seemed at first as if the burning had returned to his shoulder, mounting as the waning Small-Bright light bathed the rocks. The burning spread slowly but inexorably until his body was aflame. He tried to whimper, tried to snap at his paw and exchange this phantom, eerily frightening pain for the more understandable pain of warm blood spurting through ripped flesh. But he could not move, could not make a sound.

The rocks beneath him grew icy cold, and the cold pierced his belly and loins and struggled unevenly with the fire.

Finally, as with the snapping of a single branch holding back an avalanche, his head rose until his muzzle pointed directly overhead. The flesh of his throat strained taut and tight. He bayed. The wail echoed peak to peak until it seemed as if a strange pack had surrounded him, creeping nearer and nearer.

His pent-up frustrations released—and with them, surprisingly, his fear—he looked down....

And beheld an alien world.

Shadows deepened until he could see only the blackness of dark webbed by the silver of Small-Bright light on isolated rocks. Everything else disappeared: valley, trees, even the tumble of rocks twenty body-lengths straight below. He could see nothing.

But strangely the blindness was not a thing of fear. He rose. His joints creaked faintly in the silence. As he moved, he could hear the scrape of coarse hair against coarse hair. His breathing became ragged and frighteningly loud.

For a long time, he huddled on his haunches, his rear legs tight against his warmth, his forelegs stiff and straight. The

19

bunched muscles in his haunches quivered, rippled. He felt as if something in him were about to burst.

And then he moved again.

He balanced precariously as his forelegs—still deathly stiff and straight—rose rigidly in front of him and his hind legs suddenly bore his entire weight.

And still he rose, his eyes bulging in terror as his spine crackled and the muscles of hip and knee twisted and his taut forelegs glowed, glistened hideously in the moonlight, whitely smooth and bare.

His claws receded with the whispering of snakes in dead grass. They almost disappeared into long, narrow, soft pads that separated from each other and then wriggled slowly, singly, fluidly, like summer reeds in the riverbeds.

He swayed, caught his balance somehow, then looked down to where his hindpaws clutched at the rock.

Swept by a wave of dizziness and nausea at what he saw, he thrust his glance upward and concentrated on the ring of clouds around the Small Bright. He shivered as his lips grew parched. Uneasily, he allowed his body to lean backward until it rested against a rock. Rough granite dug into his naked back. The rock was cold and sharp.

He looked down again.

His hindlegs had lengthened. They ended in useless, flat, gross parodies of paws—hideous lumps like his front paws had become, only longer at the base, with the reed-like extensions shorter and blunter. They had no claws, no hair. The crumbling rock beneath them cut into tender flesh.

And, as if one deformity were not enough, something horrible throbbed awkwardly at the juncture of his legs. It was blunter, longer and thicker than his own, and rose against the shadows cast by moonlight against rock.

His vision blurred again and salt dripped into his mouth. For a moment, he felt numbed, dead. Sight had failed; smell had almost disappeared; taste faded to mere hints of tangy saltiness tantalizing his tongue—*soft, flat, smooth organ rubbing against nubbed teeth that could neither rend nor rip nor tear*—without betraying the secrets of its source.

He swayed, frantically slapping the useless, distorted paws against the granite. A shard sliced flesh, and he saw black blood on the rock—*his blood*—but could not smell it. He touched hand to tongue. The flavor was faint, mild, tepid. A new wave of dizziness slammed against him, and the extensions on his paws flexed like reeds and grasped again at rough places on the cliff. They held him tightly against the coolness of rock.

For a long time, he struggled in himself.

And then....

His head snapped away from the rock and he drew himself erect. The blurring and the dizziness disappeared. Drawing himself taller, he stared into the landscape below. Damp air fingered his nakedness, cooling and refreshing, stimulating his sex as he thought of the night ahead—*the death, the blood, the Power!*—until it grew heavy and pounded in tandem with the beat of his heart. The veins along his throat echoed the pulse. He stepped forward, toes curling tightly around palm-sized rocks. He moved to the cliff and poised on the razor edge and looked down. He listened, but could hear nothing.

Below, in a silvered glade tinged with the first hints of dawn, there was no movement.

They sleep—or, perhaps, not, he thought with a silent laugh. Even though his nose was not as keen as theirs, his eyes as sharp, his ears as keen, he knew they were there. He could feel them—*imagine them*—cowering in reeking dens, dreading his approach.

He laughed, out loud this time. The sound spiraled upward and echoed from the mountains.

When it died, the silence seemed darker, deeper.

His brow wrinkled, and for a moment he felt a wolfish snarl rise, then dissolve in his throat before it reached the broad, flat teeth that blocked his breath.

No matter. He lived and killed and all was as it should be.

His hand rose and touched his shoulder. There was warmth and a swelling just below the roundness of muscle. A small red scar spidered over the flesh. He pressed with one finger and grimaced when the pain flared. *A scratch,* he thought, *infection. It will pass.* And if it did not...well, nothing must hamper his mission.

And so...to work.

This time, he knew at once, the hunt would be different. Each Light before, he had awakened among the enemy to find himself hidden in a fetid hole, ready to creep out, cross the valley, almost blindly ascend the rock-strewn cliff, and pull *it* from its cache deep within the rocks—hidden where claws and paws could never find it but nimble, fragile fingers could uncover it readily. Only then would he descend and follow his chosen prey into the forest, himself no more than a wisp, a phantom, a fragment of dreams to hollow to have form. Twice a bitch had been asleep in the hole where he woke, a ready target had he had *it*; but each time he ignored her for worthier prey and for the sheer, sensual—*even sexual*—thrill of the stalk and the kill through the wilderness night.

But now, tonight...tonight he stood naked (as always) on the cliff, looking down upon the vermin. He imagined dawnlight glinting in open, frightened eyes. Perhaps they could see him as he stood here, erect and powerful, a white glistening against grey rock. If so, they would fear and cower. He breathed heavily as strength surged through him and warmth entered every cell.

A cloud scudded across his mind. He shook his head, trying to penetrate a sudden vagueness. *He* was Death. *He* prowled the nameless wastes, sustained by vague, throbbing powers that surged through his body.

He laughed, a nervous sound that swirled and twined with combinations of sounds at once both words and inarticulations of primitive emotions.

He leaped backward, into the darkness, and scrabbled blindly at the cairn of rocks. His fingers ached with the strain as they lifted rocks the size of his own torso. Once, two boulders slid together and pinched the skin of his arm. He cried in pain and held the arm up to the light. The dark patch that was blood startled him more than had the pain.

He turned again to his work. He did not stop until his probing fingers touched coldness and smoothness and hardness. He pulled it out.

It glinted in the moonlight. It felt heavy in his hand, yet oddly comfortable as his fingers caressed the trigger. He raised it arm-high, scarcely noting the twitch in his shoulders, and sighted down the barrel, picking target after target from among the shadows and firing at imaginary prey. Silver eyes glared at him from the roundness beneath the barrel.

He climbed down from the rocks. Once on the forest floor, he ran easily. His body was made for running, for leaping. His arms swung loosely at his side, one hand unclenched and relaxed, the other grasping the weapon. Once his bare foot struck a rock. The pain made him break stride for a moment, then he was himself again. This was what he lived for. This...and killing *them*.

He slowed along the ridge leading into the valley. Here he climbed carefully, since his hands and feet—*and other parts as well*—were vulnerable to sharp edges. Sliding down one rock face, he tore open the half-clotted cut on his arm. Blood oozed freshly, and he reached over and touched the blood and rubbed thick blood—*his blood*—between his fingers, curiously, as if he had never seen such a thing before. He touched a reddened fingertip to his tongue—*and for a second thirsted for more, for warmth and life and breath.* He swallowed convulsively, his throat long and white in the moon-light. His vision flickered...he stumbled...and then he was himself again, erect, wiping the blood on a rough leaf plucked from a low bush as he ran by. His stomach was knotted.

The soil beneath the ridge grew damp and spongy. The air felt cool. He ran, his mind lingering absently on thoughts of warmth and comfort and thick fur—

On him, not *around* him.

He stumbled, sprawling on the humus. His were eyes closed but his mind hovered madly between two visions (*not true cant be true isnt true*). Then the moment died and he stood in a single fluid thrust, conscious of his pride in the movement as he transformed it into a personal gesture of triumph.

He stood erect. Lesser creatures crawled.

He was Death. Lesser creatures died.

Circling a pond overgrown with reeds, he caught a glimpse of a fleeting reflection. Puzzled, suddenly halfway to the border of fear, he stopped and knelt and looked into the black waters.

And saw...a dim white form locked between insubstantial trees. He was reminded of.... Of what? He had never seen a body like this before—(*thin white body twisted bloodily against a thornbush on a treeless pass, head crushed body crushed flesh crushed blood devoured*)—yet somehow he knew instinctively, as if in a waking dream, that he had.

His stomach wrenched again.

Confused, he cried aloud, an agonized cry devoid of the earlier laughter and confidence. Behind his eyes, two visions flickered, kaleidoscopic and terrifying. The cry receded into tears.

A sound startled him. He whirled to face the forest but could see nothing until a small form—a fieldmouse? a ground squirrel? as large as a rabbit?—scuttled across the path.

He laughed silently, laughed at his fears.

As if anything could threaten *him*.

He was the power!

He returned to the hunt, moving swiftly but carefully to avoid cuts or scrapes—yet irrationally almost desiring them. Desiring the warmth of blood against his tongue, wrapping his throat with warmth.

He concentrated on the trees, the trail, the sky, and saw no more reflections in the water.

When he reached open ground, he stepped boldly into the dawn, flaunting his posture, reveling in the erect shadow that spread out to his side. This time, he would enter their domain. He would penetrate their lairs and dare the beasts cowering in shadows to attack him.

He strode toward an elevated rock in the center of the clearing. He felt their yellow eyes peering at him from all sides. He threw his head back and laughed—and the eyes blinked out, then slowly reappeared, fearful and wary.

He raised the weapon. There was a long moment of silence, then he suddenly yelled, swinging the weapon over his head, exulting in the words that coursed like sunlight through his body and exploded from his throat.

"Come out! Out of your holes and face me!"

As soon as they passed his lips, the words became crude and harsh, obscene parodies of the sounds that welled within him but still the closest to them that he could create. His throat cracked and his lips burned. Even so, the power of the sounds excited him.

And horrified *them*.

One by one, shadows crept from darker shadows until he stood at the center of a half-circle of huge, cringing, shaggy beasts. The stench was overpowering this close—the wildness, the filth. They approached until they were less than two body lengths away, then they huddled against the ground, their eyes riveted on him.

He swung the weapon again, circled it around his head until the barrel was even with his eyes, then he aimed and fired at a rock across the clearing. The rock shattered with a flash of red. The animals whirled to run, but he cried "Stay!" and they crouched down again, skittish and even more uneasy.

They did not understand words but they responded to the power of voice and will.

He played the barrel along the row of beasts. None moved, save for a silent baring of teeth in fury...or in fear. He raised his arms slowly. The swelling ached, but he ignored it. He gestured to himself, touching his bare chest with the tip of the weapon. It was hot and burned his skin but with a pain that merged with pleasure.

"I am..." he began. "I am *man*....I...."

He knew what he knew, but the words would not come. He could not articulate his essence. The single *I* extended to become more growl than speech. It spiraled wildly into a cry that was half wolf-howl, half human-exultation.

At the tension in the sound, the ring of beasts edged closer. He threw both arms outward, and the great shaggy creatures shied away from the movement.

"Back!"

They obeyed.

He tried once more to force words out, to make his lips and throat and tongue form the sounds that would fling truth into the air. But behind his eyes, two visions warred, and the sounds refused to accept the discipline of words. He tried to tangle out unspoken, unspeakable Memories, but they swirled into incoherence. He tried to speak. He was the Power. He must kill. Not just wound, but *kill*.

If he only wounded, if the flesh remained alive....

He screamed, a thin, high-pitched cry that hurt their sensitive ears as it careened from rock to rock. The pack leaped back, less from pain than from the terror it embodied.

"I...I....kill! No! *No more!*"

He turned the hot barrel of the weapon until it touched a vein throbbing in his throat. His finger tightened.

For an instant, he was bitterly aware of everything around him: the ring of beasts, the fading moon and rising dawn, cold stone beneath naked feet, rock clattering from the slope behind him.

His finger pressed the trigger.

And a body crashed against him, knocking his aim wild. The weapon flew from his hand and, glinting in the light, smashed against rock. He stumbled sideways, lost his balance, and rolled. He scrabbled frantically for a foothold, a handhold, anything so that he could stand again and fight.

One shuddering vision surfaced completely. He *would* fight. He *would* destroy the beasts.

With a hideous snarl, something struck him from behind. Claws skinned along the ridge of his spine, leaving stipples of hot blood. He twisted, shrieking nonwords as he grabbed coarse fur between his hands and pushed. Teeth ripped along his cheek. Hot, fetid breath nearly suffocated him as he thrust the squirming mass away again, then the teeth were back, on his shoulder this time, gouging out a jagged chunk of flesh where the swelling had been.

The pain spiralled into agony. Flames beyond fire spun through him, and his consciousness splintered into darkness. With a supreme effort, he rose to one knee, then fell, and struck his temple....

＊ ＊ ＊ ＊ ＊

Even before he was fully awake, he recognized the faint light. Shadowed light. Coolness. The comfortable moistness of the den. He raised his head and focused. She lay curled across from him, watching him.

His head ached sickly. Inside, he dimly felt a maddening swirl of impossible things—strange bodies, foully shaped and deformed, fragile and unsuited to the wilds. And there was a thing that sent death like thunder. And there was pain.

He tried to follow one of the flickering images but it intersected with the Memory and momentarily blunted it. He backed away. The Memory was all there was. Without it, the pack would die.

After a long time, the patterns settled and his head felt better. He tried to rise. She bared her fangs. He settled back and stared at her. After a time, she relaxed. The sleep-shadows—dreams (what was that?)—were gone. He licked the blood-matted pelt around his throbbing shoulder. There was a large wound now, deeper than before. But it smelled clean and wholesome. He tried to move the leg. It was painful but he could move it. There would be a long healing.

He sniffed carefully, then nosed the flesh, mindful of torn tissue. The knot at the center of the wound was gone. The burning and the swelling beneath the skin were gone.

He looked at her and growled hungrily.

She left.

He lay back. Most of the sleep-shadows that hovered on the edges of the Memory had already faded. Many had died. There was something about killing and death. And the shape of a dream-body reflected in a pool.

And something else.

Sounds echoed behind his closed eyes. Some were pack-sounds. But others were more...difficult. Complicated.

Frightening.

He bristled.

Sounds that stood for...that *meant*.

Here was something new.

He growled. It was an odd, low sound unlike any he had ever made before. He tried again, with a slightly different pitch. His muzzle twitched as he struggled to make the sound match one that echoed in his head.

"*Aiiiee.*"

He tried again.

"*Aiii.*"

And again.

"*I*!"

Then he rested. He could teach her. And they could teach the others. And then....

He was tired. He slept.

Around him, through the nameless forest, silence echoed, waiting for the sounds of speech.

A Midnight Shooting on

Three witnesses watched with livid horror...,
Three witnesses to the spear of bloody violence
That sliced the freeway's swollen arteries
On long hot deadly summer nights.

More unusual...all three agreed:
The screaming Volkswagen had attacked,
Thrumming past their wide-eyed gaze so closely
That the silver crucifix glinting from its window frame

Glimmered like the ghost of false hopes dead.
"I could not see the driver's face, though,"
One later murmured to the *Times*,
"The night was dark, too shadowy."

The blood-red car sped past; as yet unseen,
It drew abreast its plodding victim—
A rumbling Cadillac, long and unreflective black,
High-finned recluse from another age.

A rifle barrel slipped between glass and frame;
A gout of flame, a slice of smoke—
And the Volkswagen fled beyond the overpass
To disappear into the sheltering night.

The Cadillac shuddered, swerved,
Wallowed wildly lane to throat-constricting lane,
Slid screeching against thick concrete pilings
And, in an agony of twisting steel, died.

In a cul-de-sac where L.A. lights
Glistened like blood on mica sands,
Two teenaged lovers were not yet serious
In their petting when the shots erupted and

the Golden State Freeway

The dying Cadillac careened and crashed
Against a buttress wall not fifty feet away.
"No one left the wreck," they said, their eyes
Dead orbs of shock and pain. "No one left."

But when the cops flung back the blackness
In the Cadillac with their eight-celled flash,
Wrenched away the door with wailing squeal,
The driver's seat stretched emptily...a violated sepulchre.

The coroner examined the viscous spray of fluid
Staining crimson-washed seats and dash and glass—
"Not blood," he said, "not quite. Not blood.
Something else. But close."

Armed officers patrolled all access roads,
Searched all frontage lanes...but the Cadillac,
Long black coffin length skewed against the overpass,
Crouched empty as the vile breath of plague.

Later, hidden in the trunk, they found the bones—
Femur, humerus, half a skull bereft of brain.
All gnawed, shredded, flayed, and
Hung with rancid bits of human flesh.

Flat against the metal window frame
In line with where the rifle must have fired,
They found the slug as well—jagged spit of metal
Forensics tests affirmed as pure, untainted silver.

Black Dandelions

Black dandelions storm-heart black
Crowd the crumbling Commons wall.
Taproots crowned with grey-green
Toothy coils that curl upon themselves
Sink slowly Hellward....
Thirsty rootlets nose blindly for a draught
Of moistness where the Witchman
Lies amouldering.

They killed him first a month ago—
A blast of silver slicing lungs and heart
That blew life from his flesh.

They killed him next a fortnight past,
When flaming hawthorne pierced his skull
And crushed the convoluted grey within.

They burned his flesh until no thing remained
But ash and bone—then buried both
Two man-lengths deep beyond the Commons wall.

He waited yet another fortnight—
Buried deep, seed to Witchman seed in ashy crypt.
And now, with the full moon's lambent blast, grey
Ashes stir, burnt bones knit, moistness rises upward.
The Witchman rises...bringing with him
Lethal winds to scatter midnight Death-seeds
Among the villagers beyond the Commons wall,
Where grow profusely in the darkness,
Storm-heart black, black dandelions

Homo Lupus

Cells roil in rage beneath hot muscle slabs,
Ravening—
Cells course through veins and arteries,
Hot spheres of *Wolfishness*
Combat human corpuscles,
Devour, displace....

Like opalized Infernity,
Cells transform life to death,
Cleave one flesh
To other, alien forms,
And thirst and starve
For satiating human taste.

Night falls. Eyes close. Blood heats....
And bursts cool skin
With fangs and fur—hirsute flesh
Now hungers for its former self,
Not to restore...
But to consume.

Part Two:
Heritage of Fear

Crucifax
for Ray Garton

Crucifax—
blood blooms, nails bloom
silver petals huddling in caverns
of claw-curled palm
shadows

Blood droops
downward, carves a hillock
breast, curls a pain-tense abdomen
a map—a markery of life
untraced

Breath stops
blood stops pounds flows
severed artery heart-thrums
thoroughfares fragmented
severed

Arms arch
swan-arched embracing
back bow-burdened lungward
lunging through
darkness

Death holds its
fetid breath and will not
strike. Bruised nerves taut taunt
tissues torn and dipped like sops
in bursting blood

that pounds
and groans through bursting throats—
and dark and calm and pain and aching
silence, stillness, chill
of death

A Midnight Horror Reading
Friday, 12 May 1989

Lightning washes gruel-white into
The waiting bowl of Estes Park—
White wails to heart-beat blue as
Thunder cracks.
Cold as death itself, rain drips
On snow-scarred shingles, black in midnight shadows.
Cold as certain death itself, rain curtains
Glass rippled by the bated breath of age.

Inside, lights flicker, dim.
Listeners exhausted
      from their flights,
        from the heady ride from Denver,
      from the altitude
Shift sleepily in plastic seats.

Lights fade away
Except one blood-spot, center stage.
A heart-thrum pause.
Silence.
Sussurant rustle of folded words.
A breath.
A voice.

And ghost-hands rest solemnly on shoulders.
Darkness rises through the midnight black
      darkness darker than mere lack of living light
      darkness deeper than soft sigh of passing life
And Death now ranges unimpeded through
Self-haunted hallways,
Death
Supreme
Until the fragile dawn.

The Calling of the Dead:
A Monody

The moon skims low across night skies;
Pale stars abrade silk clouds;
Stark night rests dark on glade and park;
Black yew trees twist unbowed.

The night has fed
On daylight fled;
It is the time of madness and the Calling of the Dead.

Their fetid breath on window sill
Recalls me to wild fears—
My shrouded lamplight dies to night,
Bitter as unshed tears.

I lie abed
With horror new-bred—
It is the hour of madness and the Calling of the Dead.

They pass my opened, unchained door;
In ghostly garb they walk,
Grey-shouded forms that whisper harms,
From room to room they stalk—

They fill my head
With murmured dread—
It is the time of madness and the Calling of the Dead.

From stone-cleft haunted catacombs
They echo banshee wails,
They poison ears with acid fears....
I feel my heartthrob fail:

Dry eyes burn red,
Harsh breathing fled—
It is the hour of madness and the Calling of the Dead.

Their hissing bursts frail bonds of life—
I rise ... I stand ... I faint—
My fingers clasp their ice-fleshed grasp—
My lungs freeze with constraint.

No more abed
I, too, am led—
It is the time of madness—and I join the Summoned Dead.

39

A Pound of Chocolates
on St. Valentine's Day

1.

Most people don't even know the place exists. The few who do call it Shadow Valley, although the name appears on no maps, on no county or state registers. It is less a town or a village than a ragged patchwork of farmhouses set a quarter-mile or so apart.

It is set in a wide valley, ten miles beyond the monument at Point of the Mountains that commemorates the last Indian massacre of white settlers in the state of Idaho. In the spring the valley assumes a green veneer of prettiness that occasionally fools passing motorists. Feathery grey-green poplars skirting irrigation ditches contrast with the variegated greens and golds of corn and wheat and truck gardens. For a short time, the valley can look pretty.

But in January, everything is different.

Winds whistle through Black Willow Canyon—freezing, biting winds straight off the year-round snowcap of Mount Cleveland. They tear through bare upraised arms of emaciated poplars and gnarled, arthritic-looking boxelders and whirl across empty fields scored with skeletal stubble and clots of frozen earth the color of dessicated blood.

When there is snow, the valley attains a starkly forbidding picturesqueness—at the right time of day and from far enough away.

But when Aunt Annie died, the valley hadn't seen that much snow for over twenty years. Old man Willard's four-horse sleigh—large enough to carry fifteen merrymakers through drifts higher than their heads—hadn't moved an inch for three decades. It sat in its own ruts, shrouded in dust and decaying leaves and the acrid whiteness of bird droppings. Its wooden runners had warped away from the rusty pins that should have held them in place.

Travellers mostly don't even know they have been through Shadow Valley until they get to Oakley on the other end of the county road. They swing around Point of the Mountain, past the historical marker telling about the Great Uprising of 1895, then follow the two-lane blacktop into the valley. They might notice the old Tuttle place off to the left, its sod roof crumbling between weathered silvery posts. Or the graveyard perched on the slope like a discolored patch of lichen, faded and barren against the sagebrush. They pass the old abandoned schoolhouse crouching behind its thorny barricade of hip-high weeds. Sometimes they notice Tower Rock thrusting up on the northern crest of the mountains that enclose the valley—most times they don't.

They never notice the old house set way back from the road at the end of a driveway so overgrown and faded it can't remember when it last felt tire tracks.

That's Aunt Annie's place.

Travellers don't know about her.

They wouldn't want to.

2.

Aunt Annie wasn't my aunt, not really. A sort of shirt-tail great aunt, actually—my grandmother's half-sister. There wasn't much family left in Shadow Valley when I got the letter about Aunt Annie. Only my cousin Anna, named through some horrible mischance after Aunt Annie.

I didn't make it to the funeral. Only later in the summer, when the searing heat had baked the valley dry, and the air hung heavy over dried-up corn and wheat that looked nearly dead, could I get back to Shadow Valley.

I wish to God now that I hadn't.

Aunt Annie seemed unutterably old when she finally died. She had lived alone since her mother burned to death in a kitchen fire in 1914. The house, battered by the years of weather and neglect, stood forlornly on one of the original homesteads. Two stories of hand-cut pine Aunt Annie's father had pulled down from Mount Cleveland by horse team to build a home for his wives.

Yes, wives.

Four of them.

But only two in Shadow Valley. The other two lived up north in Canada; they had moved there long before the government in D.C. made it a crime to practice polygamy. Grandma told stories about her father's six-month trips to Aunt Naomi and Aunt Ethel. It was years before I understood what she wasn't coming right out and saying. Grandma wasn't exactly ashamed about her family—she just didn't like to talk about it.

Aunt Annie, now, she was different.

She hated her father and she hated all three of her father's other wives. Her mother had been the last, a young woman, beautiful by all accounts (you can't believe the lithograph of her hanging in its dark oak frame over the fireplace—nobody, it seems, ever walked away from an encounter with a lithographer looking like anything but a sour old witch). Now, to be fair, Great-granddad had tried to do right by all four of his families. The two wives in Canada each had a place of her own on farms separated by a measly little creek that dried up by April of each year. But the houses *were* separate.

By the time he settled in Shadow Valley, things were different. By then, Great-granddad couldn't quite swing two places. So he compromised, like so many of the old-time polygamists did.

He built two houses under one roof.

The place had two full kitchens; one has long since been turned into a pantry. Upstairs were two sets of bedrooms— six in all, three on each side of a hallway originally partitioned to make the bedrooms seem like two apartments. The partitions came down long ago, too.

And there were two front parlors.

Aunt Mattie, the first wife, insisted on that. The two other wives in Canada were all right with her, she is supposed to have said when Great-granddad began roughing out plans for the house on the Shadow Valley homestead, but no other woman would ever tell her what to do in her own parlor. So even before Aunt Annie's mother officially became part of the family, Great-granddad built the house with two parlors on the ground floor.

Aunt Mattie filled up her allotment of bedrooms easily— my grandma and her two sisters in one, four brothers in the other. Mattie's side of the house was lively, if Grandma's stories can be trusted.

The other side was much, much quieter.

There was only one child. Annie. There had been others, but they were all born dead—one stillborn, one with the umbilical cord cinched so tightly around his neck that it nearly cut through the tender flesh. Family gossip, not yet stilled by the passing years, also whispered of hideous deformities.

At any rate, there was "Aunt" Rachel, alone in spite of the growing crowds around her. I remember Grandma tell-

44

ing me about Rachel sitting hour after hour in her parlor, Annie playing quietly with a box of old buttons and a needle and a string with no knot at the end—it curled like a snake back into the button box, and almost as quickly as the large, hand-carved buttons slipped onto her string they fell again into the pile at the bottom of the box. Annie never seemed to notice that she was making no progress at all.

Rachel hated everything about her life. Everything except Annie. The baby received all of the love the woman had to offer. Maybe too much of it.

And Rachel always complained, mostly about not having things. By the time Grandma can remember clearly (she was Mattie's youngest, born in 1895, about three years after Rachel finally delivered a living child), Great-granddad was having a rough time. He had to quit his trips to Canada. He had no money for them any more, and besides, the kids up there were almost fully grown. He sold both farmhouses eventually. I don't know what happened to the wives and kids.

But with eight youngsters still in Shadow Valley, he was pressed to find the wherewithal to care for them. Grandma told stories of sparse winters and cold nights when the three girls would huddle together beneath a single worn quilt. Their teeth would chatter as loudly as the wind and screaming snow outside.

Aunt Rachel, of course, had only one child to care for, so she got less than Aunt Mattie—much less than she felt she deserved. She had her parlor, her kitchen, her suite of empty bedrooms so cold that beards of ice caked the windows in the dead of winter. Two of the rooms were empty, since Annie always slept in her mother's bed. Mattie envied those two empty rooms whenever she saw her four boys cramped into a room barely large enough for two, but she never mentioned them to Rachel. Rachel guarded the

45

rooms with the acquisitiveness a dragon feels for its hoard.

But Rachel believed to the bottom of her heart that she deserved more.

She took her bitterness out on the others.

Great-granddad died in 1910 when a horse-drawn plow skittered over the frozen earth one day in early spring and sliced him open from throat to groin. Rachel had warned him that the ground was too hard. As he stomped out the kitchen door, she stared at him with an expression the rest of the family grew to understand, to hate ... and to fear. She had warned him but he wouldn't listen.

Over the years she warned others as well, about many things. The lucky ones listened.

Edmond went next, less than a month after his father's burial. In those years before innoculations and adequate medical treatment, *diphtheria* was a word that struck dread into every mother's heart. Grandma told me once about watching her brother choke to death on a cot in the kitchen, his face twisted in agony, his throat grey and dead-looking even before the last of life left his body. Rachel had warned him about going fishing with Joe Miller, the neighbor boy who showed the first signs of the disease the night they came home with the first catch of the year. Joe Miller was dead three days later. Edmond lasted a week.

And then he was dead, too.

Albert went that summer. At twenty-two he suddenly had to assume the mantle of eldest son and man of the house. He took his responsibilities seriously. One day in early June, he hitched the team to the wagon, sharpened his axe, and headed into the ranges below Mount Cleveland to cut wood for winter. Rachel warned him not to go alone. She warned him about rattlers and rocky trails and trees that fell the wrong way and sharp axes that sometimes willfully severed human flesh instead of timber.

46

She warned him.

The team returned just after supper that night. The buck-wagon was half full of cut ash—it made the hottest fires, Albert knew. The search parties didn't find Albert's crushed remains for a week; by that time, there was little left of his face and hands and feet, and the flesh along his rib cage had been ripped off in ragged strips—but there was enough left to see the hideous gash that had nearly severed his right leg, and the blood-stained axe lying next to the body in a pool of crusted brown that was Albert's blood.

Rachel nodded once when she heard the news. She had warned him.

Aunt Mattie was pretty old by that time, a good twenty years older than Rachel. For a while, she tried to keep the farm going, but she didn't have the heart for it. Finally, she just picked up and left. She moved herself and what was left of her family down the road to Oakley where she had folks. Somehow, Rachel found the money to buy the place from Mattie—money from her family maybe, although no one knew where she came from or who her folks were. The money was there, though, right to the dollar to meet the price Mattie had put on the house, the farm, the animals. Rachel paid, and Mattie left.

None of Mattie's kids came back to Shadow Valley except Grandma, when she got married.

The move left Rachel alone with the house ... and with Annie.

She locked up most of the rooms the way they were on the day Mattie left. No one I know ever went into the bedrooms on Mattie's side of the house until the day Aunt Annie died. Rachel used Mattie's parlor. Oh yes, she moved her heavy Victorian plush couch in front of the west window (she had always coveted that window) and spent hours watching the sunsets in the summer. She re-arranged her furniture throughout the ground floor; she even sent away to Chicago and New York for new pieces, things that Great-Grandpa had not allowed her to buy.

I suppose she was finally happy.

And every February 14, the postman hand delivered a one-pound box of chocolates.

At first they came by special carriage from Burley, the nearest town of any size. Most of the people in Shadow Valley figured that Rachel sent them herself. After what she considered years of neglect, she must have needed something tangible to prove something to her self—so every February 14 there came a gaudy box, stiff with ribbons and satin and filled with chocolates. She let everyone she spoke to know about the chocolates, but no one ever tasted any. Unless it was Annie.

Rachel and Annie lived together for a few years, both of them increasingly reclusive—just the aging woman and a pretty young thing, slender as a willow. At first there was a good deal of sympathy for the two women, isolated and alone. But sympathy was rapidly replaced by caution, and caution by avoidance.

There was something wrong at Aunt Annie's place.

It took a while for the rest of Shadow Valley to notice, but there was definitely something wrong.

First off, the animals died.

Not of a sudden, nothing like that. Maybe even some of them just wandered off. Probably the wolves that still haunted the lower mountains got a few that first winter.

But when Old Man Willard drove out in the spring of 1911, there wasn't any stock at all. He puttered around in the barn some, taking his sweet time collecting the odds and ends of ironwork he was buying from Rachel. When he got back to his place that night, he seemed much quieter than usual. Four years later, after he died, his wife first mentioned the dreams that plagued his final years—they had begun the night after that visit. He had never gone out to Rachel's again.

No one ever did.

Well, not quite. After Grandma married and moved back to Shadow Valley, she drove out once or twice to see Rachel. She never went beyond the house but even from there she could tell that the place was going downhill fast—fences falling over, the barn looking like it was ready to collapse with the next winter's snows (even though it stood until 1934, when it burned to the ground), the wagons and harrows and plows rusted, cracking, and useless.

Things like that.

And Rachel had changed, Grandma said. Grandma was well into her seventies when she finally spoke to me about all of this.

"Gone to fat, she was," Grandma said with more than a touch of satisfaction giving her voice a saccharine whining quality so unlike her. "Gone to fatness and softness. Big, too. Big as a house. And her always so proud of her figure. Must've been them chocolates."

"Chocolates?" I remember asking, a boy entranced by a brief vision of a world long dead.

She studied me over the frames of her bifocals.

"Chocolates," she repeated, her voice harsh.

I couldn't get any more from her, except that Rachel had become monstrously fat by the time the war came, 1914, the year she reached across the old wood-burner for a pot of oatmeal one morning and dragged her sleeve across the heated surface. The ancient ecru lace she always wore at the cuff flickered into flame, and before she could move an inch toward the bucket of water that was supposed to stand right next to the stove but was unaccountably clear across the kitchen on the counter next to the Hoosier cabinet, she was a screeching pillar of fire, her dress burning off her body in an instant, her flesh sizzling and popping and cracking like the strips of bacon curling in the frying pan not half a foot away.

The floor was a little scorched, but Annie was able to put the fire out with no other damage to the house.

Of course, no one was there to see what really happened; everyone relied on what Annie could tell them through her tears and her shock. Annie repeated again and again that she had warned her mother about fire. But Rachel just wouldn't listen.

They buried what was left of Rachel three days later in the old church, the hand-cut rock one, not the brick one that went up in 1952. Grandma said that the casket was closed—probably just as well, considering. But some of the folks said that even under the circumstances, it was a mighty small casket for a woman of Rachel's size.

3.

They buried Rachel, and Annie—now a girl of seventeen—went back alone to the old house. To my knowledge, no one ever saw her again, face to face, except Grandma. For some reason that not even Grandma ever understood, she and Annie got along well. Maybe they were close enough in age, maybe Annie was envious of Grandma and her new husband and wanted to experience Grandma's life vicariously through the stories Grandma told. Whatever the reason, Grandma would drive out to the old place every once in a while, whipping the buggy team along with a practiced hand. She always went alone.

They would sit in the west parlor—Mattie's parlor—and talk about this and that, nothing special, then Annie would get a far away look in her eyes and Grandma would hitch herself up and say "Thanks for the nice afternoon, Annie," and leave.

Now, I got most of this from Grandma in the year or two before she died. She wasn't really that sharp any more, of course, and I wouldn't swear by all of what she said, but it's more than anyone else ever knew for sure about Aunt Annie. Until she finally opened up to me, I don't think Grandma had spoken to anyone in Shadow Valley about those drives.

Well, life went on, as it always does. Grandma had children. Some died, two lived—my mother and my Aunt Mae. Grandpa died a lonely death somewhere in the Pacific in 1944; no body was ever returned, so the marble stone in the Shadow Valley graveyard stands atop an empty casket. My mother died in childbirth. I was born in Shadow Valley, in the old house Grandpa built the first year he was married. Aunt Mae died in 1970, when her only child Anna was only three. Grandma took the little girl in.

For her last few years, Grandma seemed even closer to Annie than before. She drove out at least once a week, until in 1977 she fell and broke her hip getting out of the car after one of the visits. She seemed angry as she slammed the car door and swiveled toward the icy sidewalk. Her foot skidded out from under her and she slammed against her hip. The sound crackled through the brittle-cold air. She was almost ninety at the time. She was strong and feisty, but it took only that one slip to put her out of things for good. She died the next year.

Anna moved in with Grandpa's only surviving nephew—and that's when things started going wrong again.

All we knew of Aunt Annie at the time was that she had become as huge as her mother. Grandma wouldn't say much more—certainly not to outsiders, certainly not to the child, Anna. No one ever went out to Aunt Annie's place, except the Tuttle boy, who left a case of groceries on a wagon (or a sled, if it was winter) that was always just inside the front gate each Monday morning. No one saw Aunt

Annie, even though some of us kids took it as a mark of on-coming manhood to stake out the wagon and watch for her. But something always happened—a sudden storm, a cow bellowing for help in a field across the road, something to draw our attention from the wagon for a second, and then it would be gone. I think I almost saw her once, or her shadow, a great bloated wash of darkness moving through the trees surrounding the house.

Perhaps I only imagined it.

4.

The only time I actually even saw the house itself, the ex-perience ended in tragedy.

It must have been around 1965, when Grandma was still making her weekly trips. I was up for the summer, and my friend Roy and I were sleeping over at his house, about half-way down the road between Grandma's and Aunt Annie's. It was hot and sticky that night, and sleep was long in com-ing. We talked until late, then decided to play Huckleberry Finn and sneak out for an adventure. Even though his folks were probably fast asleep, he insisted that we climb down the arbor alongside his second-floor window. The thin wooden slats creaked and grumbled with our weight but eventually our feet touched ground. I don't think either of us had any clear ideas about where to go, what to do. We started walking down the moon-drenched road, talking aim-lessly in conspiratorial whispers, kicking pebbles with the sides of our sneakers.

"Sure is hot," I said, wiping sweat from my brow even though it had to have been almost midnight.

"Hey," Roy said all of a sudden. "Let's go swimming."

I wasn't sure. It was late and in spite of the bright moon-light, the shadows lurking under the trees were impenetrably dark. Pool water would be dark, too, mysterious with a bottomless blackness that would reflect the night sky. I was enough of a city boy that I wasn't quite sure about a lot of things Roy took for granted, but I couldn't let on to Roy. He and I had palled around every summer since his folks moved to Shadow Valley seven years before, and even though we saw each other only a month or two in a year, he was probably my closest friend.

"Well ... okay." It was not a whole-hearted, total commitment, but I figured it would be enough to get me by.

"There's this great place, just over the rise," he said.

We walked a bit further.

He cut away from the road and followed a narrow path through a stand of boxelders that seemed skeletal and ghostly in the filtered light.

I saw the house first. Its four broken chimneys thrust up like decaying teeth against the moonlit sky.

I swallowed, hard.

"Uh...that's...that's Aunt Annie's place," I said.

"Yeah," Roy said. He was trying to sound nonchalant, but his voice cracked at the last moment, breaking the illusion. "Yeah, so what."

Now you've got to remember that Roy was my friend, that his family had only lived in the valley for few years, buying one of the old pioneer places and turning it into a paying farm. I knew him, and I knew them, and I trusted them. But they weren't family.

I should have said something, God knows I wish to this day that I had. I should have pleaded cowardice, anything to keep from taking another step toward that house, but I didn't. Aunt Annie was *Family*.

"Well," I began, weakly enough.

"Come on, don't chicken out. It's not like it's a haunted house or anything. We don't even have to get that close to it. There's a pond out behind the shed. You can see it from the top of the hill. The water looks pretty deep. It'll be great."

He took off. I followed.

We skirted the house, all right, getting only close enough to see that the windows were as dark and close and non-reflecting as if they had been draped in death-crepe. There wasn't a suggestion of light anywhere. Even the moon seemed to darken when we stepped out from the protective shadows of the boxelders and stood for a moment in the open space between the house and the shed next to the spot where the barn had burned. Then we ducked across what once might have been a lawn and disappeared into shadows again.

I think Roy must have felt something, because as soon as we were hidden behind half a dozen man-sized trunks, Roy said, "Hey, let's...."

Then he broke off and looked at me. He might have seen the relief that flooded through me at his words, because he seemed to change his mind. His voice took on a new tone and he squared his thin shoulders. "Let's go on. Last one in's a rotten egg."

He ran toward the black, swelling shadow that was the shed and disappeared around the side. I followed more slowly. I couldn't keep from glancing over my shoulder at the dark windows, watching for a flicker of drapery, a hint of match held against the hand-twisted wick of an old-fashioned tallow candle.

I watched, and slowly followed Roy.

And then I heard the sound like a stifled whimper. It was soft, low, agonized, but it seemed to echo and re-echo like a drawn-out death-scream in the absolute silence of the night.

I froze. I wanted to make my legs go on, make them skirt the side of the shed and bear me to whatever had made that sound, but they wouldn't listen to me.

I couldn't move.

A second sound—louder this time, more ponderous and infinitely more threatening—shattered my stasis.

"Roy!" I yelled, and without thinking I careened around the shed.

Roy was naked. His clothing was scattered in a ragged line from the edge of the shed to the edge of the pond. It looked as if he had toed out of his sneakers (neither of us wore socks that night), then pulled off pants and T-shirt and undershorts on the run and, without pausing to think about how dangerous it might be, dived long and flat into the still black midnight waters of the pond.

Even from a distance, the light was bright enough for me to see that his head was crushed.

He must have struck a rock, then somehow found enough life to crawl out onto the bank and die.

I stood there, staring, numb, watching the moonlight glisten on his blood as it pooled beneath his head and shoulders and sank into the dark soil.

Only later, much later, after I had fallen to my knees and vomited until it felt my guts rip loose; only after I ran home to Grandma's and woke Dad and Grandma with my wild shrieks and heaving, gasping breaths that threatened to become uncontrollable spasms; only after Dad raced out, dressed only in his undershorts, and drove like a madman down the road while I waited in the kitchen with Grandma, my body trembling and threatening to let go of its tenuous grasp on consciousness; only when Dad returned far more slowly and walked into the kitchen and dropped heavily into the chair and took the phone from its cradle on the wall and slowly dialed Roy's folk's number—only after all of that did I remember three things.

First, even though the night was so silent that I could hear the *swish swish* of my sneakered feet in the stubbly grass, I hadn't heard Roy dive into the water.

Second, his back and legs were dry when I saw him. The moon reflected wetly from the blood pulsing from the hideous wound on his head, but not from white skin as dry and pale as ancient parchment.

And third, I had seen something. A huge shadow that disappeared beneath the trees the instant I came around the side of the shed.

That last memory was tenuous, fragmented, and I no sooner touched it than I let it go.

There couldn't have been anything. I must have imagined it in the instant of shock.

No one saw Aunt Annie the whole time between Dad arriving at the pond and Roy's burial in the graveyard halfway up the hill on the other side of the valley. She didn't come out of her house when the county sheriff pulled up in his patrol car and looked at the pond. She didn't answer when he knocked at the door to ask if she had seen or heard anything the night Roy died. She spoke to him later on the telephone from Grandma's kitchen—two hushed minutes of him asking questions, her apparently answering with a curt, whispered "yes" or "no," then him hanging up the phone with an odd look of frustration on his face.

But there never seemed to be any real question that Roy's death was more than a horrible accident. From the bank, in the bright light of day, the sheriff could even see the outline of the rock that must have killed Roy.

So my best friend was buried. Aunt Annie did not attend the funeral. No one expected her to. But when Grandma came back from visiting Annie later the next week, she shooed me outside angrily and wouldn't speak a word to Dad or me until after dinner that night—a dinner that had to have been the worst she ever cooked in her life. The roast was burned, the mashed potatoes thin and sour, the gravy heavy and clotted with lumps of flour. Even then, hours after her return from Aunt Annie's, I saw spots of high color in Grandma's cheeks and flecks of what might have been anger—or a deep, abiding fear—in her eyes.

But that's the past. Roy is only a memory.

My cousin Anna is still here. Now she is the important one.

5.

When Grandma died, like I said before, Anna moved in with Grandpa's only nephew and his family. She was about eleven at the time.

Seven years passed.

I visited only rarely, and then alone. Dad refused to return to the valley after one last trip for Grandma's funeral. Three years later, he died.

That left just Anna and me—all that remained of Grandma's family.

For most of that time, Anna's life passed uneventfully. She suffered through several schoolgirl crushes. She broke an arm falling out of the oak tree behind the house she was living in.

Then last fall, the dreams began.

She could not exactly remember them, she would explain when Uncle Evan or Aunt Vera would rush to her side and waken her from the dreams that left her screaming, sweating, and panting as raggedly as if she had just run a mile. "I don't know, I don't know," she would repeat over and over, until Vera wanted to shake her out of sheer frustration.

Night after night, the dreams came and Anna would scream, and Evan and Vera would rush to her side.

After a while only Evan came. Vera lost patience with her.

As the nights passed, Anna became listless, not quite sick but certainly not well. She lost weight.

It's hard to believe that now.

Anyway, one night in mid-January, she screamed her way out of the dream again, but this time was different.

"She's dead! She's dead!"

When Evan tried to calm her, she rapidly grew even more hysterical. She wept violently and pulled at her hair as if there were something caught in it.

Finally, though, she was able to talk.

"She's dead, Uncle Evan," she said through harsh gasps.

"Who, honey? Who?"

"Aunt Annie."

"What?"

"She's dead. I know it. We've got to get out there. Now!"

She was out of bed before Evan had a chance to argue. He tried to make her lie down again, but she threw a heavy robe over her shoulders and headed for the door.

"I'm going, Uncle Evan. I'll walk if I have to, but I'm going. Now."

When Vera met her in the hall and started to say something, Anna swept past her as if the woman did not exist. Vera stared at Anna, then transferred her stare to Evan as he rushed out of the girls' bedroom—hair still awry from sleep, his feet bare and bluish from the cold—and grabbed Vera's arm and propelled her to the kitchen.

Anna was already bundled up in boots, a heavy knee-length coat, a muffler, and a hat. Her hand was on the doorknob.

"Wait, Anna," Evan said. "We're coming too."

Vera looked at him questioningly, but he said no more.

Ten minutes later they were barrelling down the snow-dusted road at midnight in Evan's old Chevy, their breath frosting in the cold. Evan was still half numb from being awakened abruptly, Vera was stonily silent, and, huddled tightly in a corner of the back seat, Anna began whimpering like a child.

Evan took the turnoff to Aunt Annie's so fast that the snowtires lost traction and the car skewed sideways, its front fender grazing one of the boxelders.

"Evan!" Vera screamed. Anna didn't seem to notice. The whimpering was deeper now, and if Vera and Evan hadn't been so intent on what was happening to the car, they would have felt their blood chill at the sound.

Even when they were safely back on the driveway, they almost didn't make it to the house. The ice-shrouded grass in the middle of the drive had been drifted over with loose snow, and more than once the motor lugged and whined before the bumper finally broke through a ridge of snow and the car lurched forward another few feet.

It took ten minutes more to negotiate the rest of driveway, but they finally made it.

Anna was out of the car before Even killed the engine.

"Anna," he called harshly from the car. "You wait for me!"

Surprisingly, she did. She stood just to the right of the front door, not moving until Evan stumped up the three steps to the porch, followed by Vera.

The front door was unlocked. Evan turned the knob and pushed the splintered pine door open.

Inside, it was pitch black. And it smelled. A musty smell, like a root cellar that hadn't been aired for decades. Underneath the mustiness lay another smell, dark and pungent, that Evan couldn't place but that he didn't like at all.

"Aunt Annie," he called. "It's me. Evan. You awake?"

There was no answer.

Evan reached through for the light plate he figured must be next to the door. His hand slid up and down the wall for a long time, his fingers searching for the switch.

"Damn, where's the light," he mumbled.

"She doesn't have electricity," Anna murmured back.

He stared at the girl, then spoke to Vera.

"Bring me the flashlight from the glove compartment."

Vera started to say something, then thought better of it and tramped back through the snow to the car. They could hear the *click click click* as the hot engine cooled rapidly.

"You two go back to the car and wait there," Evan said to Anna when Vera handed him the flash.

"No," Anna said. "I can't. I've got to go in with you."

He looked at her, shrugged, and turned on the flashlight.

Something scuttled across the carpet and disappeared into the darkness at the end of the entry hall. Evan stepped in. Anna followed, then Vera.

The doors on the right—the ones that led to Rachel's old parlor—were closed tightly. But the ones on the left were open an inch or two. Evan pulled on one and shivered as the old wood slid away, baring a deep pit of blackness. He flashed the light inside.

Whenever Rachel's daughter had died, it was recent. The body wasn't discolored, hadn't started to decay. Aunt Annie sat on the old Victorian sofa, her body so huge that it hardly seemed possible for the couch to support her dead weight. She was swathed in the remains of some ancient gown that hung in grey folds over her body.

60

She seemed peaceful.

Anna walked past Evan. The flashlight caught her out-line and flung it onto the wall opposite. The shadow danced and jittered as Evan's hand shook—from cold as much as from shock—until it seemed possessed, demonic.

Anna laid the back of her hand on Aunt Annie's cheek.

"It's cold. Like ice."

Evan approached her and drew her away from the body.

"Come on, we've got to get home. We'll call from there."

"Call?"

"Hospital in Burley. Sheriff. The mortuary. Whoever."

When they left, they carefully closed the door to the par-lor. Aunt Annie rested for the last time on the sofa in Mattie's parlor, beneath the western window.

6.

The next day, an hour or so after the hearse from the Quint Mortuary in Burley (who had buried Shadow Valley's dead for thirty years) removed the body, Vera came with a couple of other older women who had spent their adult lives wondering about Aunt Annie and her house and what might lie inside.

They were going to "take care of things," now that Aunt Annie was finally gone.

For the second time in two days, for only the second time since 1914, someone other than Rachel, Annie, or Grandma entered the house.

The women entered the open doors of Mattie's parlor first. The room was immaculate. Whatever else Annie had become in her old age, no one could fault her housekeeping. There was not a speck of dust, not a whisper of dirt. The room was like a museum showpiece. Even the ninety-year-old wooden legs of the ornately carved Victorian sofa—now bereft of their weighty burden—gleamed softly in the filtered light.

The doors opposite—opening into what had been Rachel's parlor—were closed and locked. Vera tugged at the knob once or twice and thought she felt the old mechanism inside weaken, but by unspoken consensus the women filed down the hallway instead and disappeared into the rear of the house.

The kitchen was as sterile as the rest of the house. The table and counters were starkly bare, gleaming in the bright sunlight that cut through clean windows. The cupboard doors were closed tightly. When Vera and the others opened them, they discovered only half a box of crackers tucked in one corner of the far cupboard. In the smaller one to the right of the sink they found a single chipped plate and one ceramic mug.

The drawers were empty as well, except for one table knife, one fork, and one spoon in the silverware drawer. In the next drawer over, they found a long, sharp bread knife and a spoon large enough to serve as a ladle.

Two pots—scrubbed inside and out—sat on the rear of the antique wood-burning stove that had survived the inferno that Rachel had become and had still served her daughter almost three quarters of a century later.

Other than the box of crackers, there was no food in the kitchen. And none in the pantry across the hall either—in what had once been Rachel's kitchen.

One bedroom upstairs had been used. The mattress sagged where Annie's bulk had lain on it for so many years. A single wardrobe held two ragged dresses. Two hand-stitched quilts so old that the material in the patchwork tops had faded to a uniform brown lay folded at the foot of the bed.

There was no mirror, nothing on the wall except three old prints so washed out by time that they seemed more ghostly memories than pictures.

The other bedrooms were empty. The doors were closed but unlocked. Inside, there was nothing. No carpets, no beds, no wardrobes, no paper on the splintered wood walls.

Nothing.

That left only one room to explore. Rachel's parlor.

Standing before the locked sliding doors, Vera felt a moment's pang. She wasn't sure whether they should try to force it or wait for later, but old Mrs. Hodgfield shouldered past her. Now that Annie was gone, Myrtle Hodgfield was oldest inhabitant of the valley and as stubborn as the mules her husband bred until one kicked him in the head in 1929 and sent him spinning into a better world. With a *humph* she took a knob in each hand and yanked.

The lock gave way so abruptly that Myrtle Hodgfield almost tumbled into the room. The other women were pressing close behind her, Vera leading the pack.

Halfway open, the doors shuddered to a halt. The wood creaked and groaned but the women grabbed the doors and pulled. Whatever had obstructed the doors gave way and the heavy panel slid the rest of the way into the walls with a rustled whispering like dry winter snow.

The women entered Rachel's parlor.

It stank.

The walls were hung with peeling wallpaper in a design not made since the turn of the century. The floor was so littered with papers that none of the women could tell if there was hardwood beneath or carpeting. They could see yellowed newspapers, old circulars advertising products that disappeared before the second World War, crumpled Grange bulletins announcing meetings scheduled for sometime in 1939.

Myrtle Hodgfield took a step toward the center of the room. Beneath the papers stacked up along the wall, something scuttled away.

Myrtle Hodgfield shrieked and jerked back. Her scream—and the sudden backward pressure of her bulk—forced the others to retreat suddenly into the hall.

Vera muttered under her breath something that might have been "Lived on a farm for seventy-eight years and scared of a rat!" had she not been afraid of what Myrtle Hodgfield would say if she had heard. Instead, Vera contented herself with mumbling and stalked into the room, her pride and dignity dented both by Myrtle's preceding her there and because one of the woman had stepped on her toe as well. Vera walked across the papers—gingerly, to be sure—and stopped at the dark oak highboy against the far wall.

It was stacked with boxes.

Boxes gaudy with satin and ribbon, reeking of rotting paper and old glue and something else, heavy and cloying.

Vera opened one.

Chocolates. The whole box was full of chocolates, with only one piece missing.

She opened another box.

One piece missing.

She began tossing covers right and left, pawing through the stacks of boxes.

Chocolates, all of them missing a single piece.

She noticed what looked like tiny teeth marks scratched across some—mice, she thought, and shuddered at the thought of vermin running freely across a parlor highboy. But most of the candies were untouched even though they had turned chalky with age and some were dried and crumbling into the boxes.

She turned and stared at the other women.

Then she turned back and began counting the boxes, one by one. There were seventy gaudy Valentine's Day boxes. And seventy pieces of chocolate missing. No more. No less.

Underneath the candy boxes lay other boxes, filled with old photographs and prints, most of them family portraits although no one present could identify any of the faces. The women gingerly carried the boxes of picture out to the back-yard and burned them in the incinerator. But Vera stacked the boxes of chocolate neatly in one corner.

Later, when asked why she had done something so obviously odd, Vera couldn't explain.

7.

Aunt Annie stayed in the Burley mortuary for two days. Evan arranged to have the body returned to Shadow Valley on the afternoon before the funeral and set up in Mattie's parlor. It wasn't much of a viewing by Shadow Valley standards but a few people came, more out of curiosity than anything else.

Evan was there, of course, with Vera and Anna. Anna said little. She sat on the Victorian sofa beneath the western window and stared, perhaps at the monstrous dark oak coffin on a bier in the middle of the room, perhaps somewhere into her own secret nightmares.

About five o'clock, Evan and Vera decided it was time to go home. Anna asked to wait there for a while. After all, Aunt Annie had been her last remaining relative in Grandma's family (except for me, of course).

They let her.

And they will grieve for that choice forever.

Anna sat there, in the old sofa, while the January night closed in more deeply. She sat, unmoving.

Evening passed into night. About nine o'clock, she stood and crossed the room, perhaps trailing one hand across the polished surface of the closed casket. She opened the doors into the hallway. The icy air billowed around her from the unheated hall. Then she closed the doors behind her, crossed over and opened the doors into Rachel's parlor.

It was dark inside the room, and bitterly cold, but Anna didn't notice. She walked around the parlor, touching the ragged wallpaper, fingering the hand-carved oak mantle-piece made decades before by Great-granddad for his youngest wife. The time-faded lithograph of Rachel—young but dour and stern, almost forbidding—glowered from above the fireplace.

The women had cleaned out most of the papers, burning them indiscriminately, but Anna could still see movement along the floorboards as mice—no, she decided, as *rats* scuttled about, searching vainly for their old hiding places. In spite of the comings and goings of the past days, the place smelled musty and dead

Anna walked completely around the room. She studied every details of the wainscotting, every angle and curve of the carvings on the highboy, every polished surface of the heavy oak table in the center of the room.

Then she walked to the far wall. She lifted up the top box of chocolates, crushing a faded satin bow as she tore off the cover. She took a single piece of the candy and, as if not noticing its dusting of white mold or the scratches on its top surface, placed it into her mouth.

She bit down.

The candy tasted...heavy, chalky, dark with secrets. The soft center had crystalized long before and crunched as she chewed. Her throat rasped, suddenly dry and tight, then something in the chocolate registered in her brain and her saliva flowered, swirling around the crumbling stuff, drenching it and making it creamy and rich and thick again.

She heard a noise....

She stopped chewing, the open box hanging at a precipitous angle from her hand.

She listened.

Nothing.

She straightened the box just before half a dozen of the pieces threatened to fall out. She took another piece, another, then three at a time, barely stopping to chew or taste, swallowing them as if they were life-giving breath itself.

Without a hint of warning, the double doors into Mattie's parlor slid open. Anna barely noticed until she heard the odd sound again and turned.

The coffin in the center of the room was still closed. But filaments of light floated above it, glimmered in the darkness of Mattie's parlor, then spun through the air, across the hallway, and into Rachel's parlor. Anna watched entranced, a thin dribble of chocolate staining her chin.

The filaments continued to spin into Rachel's parlor. And now the coffin *was* moving, a faint vibration, not quite a flutter of the heavy wood, but enough.

Anna opened her mouth to scream. Her teeth were stained brown with melted chocolate.

The filaments swirled faster, stifling her scream as they solidified and swirled into a column, a pillar, a form, vague at first but rapidly taking shape. More and more light filaments sped from the coffin, as if the dead and polished wood were giving up its own essence to create... something else.

Rachel.

She stood imperious, eyes seventy-five-years dead still blazing crimson, lips curled over rotted teeth, one skeletal hand pointing toward Anna.

And then she...*it*...was Annie, not yet bloated beyond the human. Still slender, beautiful. As she had been just before Rachel's horrible death.

Then it was Rachel again. Annie. Rachel.

Each time it spun through an identity, it became sharper, more explicitly defined. Even through her terror, Anna could see the long, sharp fingernails descending from each fingertip. She could see each hair on the hideous apparition's head as it shifted faster and faster.

Annie. Rachel. Annie Rachel AnnieRachel*annierachel*....

It moved toward Anna. It reached for her, and the illusion shattered and Rachel and Aunt Annie dissolved into something else, something hideous, composed of rotting cloth like funeral shrouds, and blood-sodden bones, and black decaying flesh, and teeth like fire-blackened stumps, and *things* that moved in and out, around the bones, beneath the tattered clothing. When something like a rat—but larger, with eyes like embers—crawled out of the mouth and sat perched on the remnants of a jaw, Anna screamed and fell to the floor, senseless.

8.

They found her there at midnight. Evan and Vera came for her, worried when telephone calls to her few friends revealed that she wasn't anywhere else in the valley. They drove out and rushed in through the wide-open doorway, Evan's flashlight flickering like a ghost on the wallpaper of the entry hall.

Anna was sitting stiffly where they had left her, in the Victorian sofa beneath the western window in Mattie's parlor. Everything else was as it had been.

Almost.

Aunt Annie's casket lay open, its rose satin lining a blood-like stain in the brightness.

Her body, thin to the point of emaciation, lay stretched on the oak table in Rachel's parlor.

The withered lips were crusted with something rich and brown and creamy. A rat perched on the body nibbled at the sweetness of the lips.

Vera screamed.

9.

Anna seemed to be in shock but she recovered quickly. She could remember nothing, she told them after the funeral. She could remember only sitting on Aunt Annie's sofa, thinking. And then she must have slept.

She wasn't surprised when the lawyers from Burley told her about the will. A rather nice estate, including the house with two parlors and the farm itself.

Against the strenuous objections of both Evan and Vera, Annie moved into the house with the month.

That was what finally brought me home again.

Evan and Vera were worried. They hadn't seen Anna at all since the move. It had been four months, and they were now more than worried.

I drove out to Anna's the afternoon I arrived.

Even though there was still no telephone in the house—and no electricity, for that matter—she knew I was coming. She met me on the porch and invited me in to sit in Mattie's parlor. She looked well enough but had put on a lot of weight since I had seen her last—not too much, not yet, but still it was there.

We talked for a while, a desultory conversation that carefully skirted anything important. Then she leaned over and touched my knee.

"We're the last, aren't we. The last of Rachel's line."

"No," I said. "We're not even related to Rachel. She was only Grandma's...."

Anna cut me off with a quick gesture.

"I'm going to live here, you know," she said, with a vehemence that startled me. "I'm going to live here forever, and never want for anything, and have my own parlor."

And then she leaned even closer, her breath hot and fetid in my face, and with a conspiratorial smile that chilled me and sent my head spinning, she told me what had happened on the night she stayed alone with Aunt Annie's body.

When she finished, she sat back, her eyes sparkling with a vicious delight that still haunts me. I stared. It was beyond belief, and yet I believed it.

She shivered once, then shook her head as if to clear it, and then she was Anna again, young and beautiful.

She stood up abruptly.

"Good-bye," she said, holding out her hand in a gesture that struck me as curiously old fashioned. And then I understood that she was saying good-by forever. I would not be welcome in that house again.

"Anna," I began.

"No," she said sharply. "And don't try to talk about what you've heard. We're family; they're outsiders. Family keeps its secrets."

She laughed, a hideous and frightening laugh that seemed to come from a body much larger than hers, much older and more acquainted with evil.

"Of course, even if you did say something," she added, "no one would believe you."

"I... I...." I couldn't speak.

"Don't try," she said. "I warn you. Believe me. Don't try."

Without another word, I left the parlor.

10.

I've not returned to Shadow Valley.

Nor shall I ever.

Nor have I married. I don't intend to take any chances. One of my children might be a girl, young and slender and bright and beautiful.

And something...*final*...might happen to me and to my wife, and our child would leave our home to live with her only living relative.

In Shadow Valley. With Cousin Anna.

I wouldn't want my daughter to see on her table what I saw on Anna's when I left.

A brand-new box of chocolates, wrapped in an old-fashioned box that was already coated with a thin layer of dust but was still gaudy with satin and ribbons.

It sat open on a table in the parlor.

With one piece missing.

On the First Outdoor Testing
of a Man-Made Bacterium in a
Strawberry Patch in California

Them strawberries was big that spring—
bigger even than them my Gram remembered,
them what she had to slice in half
to make 'em fit into a Mason jar.

And sweet!—sweeter 'n anything.
We musta ate a flat ourselfs that night,
strawberries 'n' stale milk, but better
for our havin' snuck 'n' plucked 'n' got away.

That's what done it, them whitecoats said,
later, when they come.
We waren't s'posed to heist 'em from *that* field
they said—we shouldn'da broke in.

But we did—we didn't know they was
special bred or somethin' like. We picked,
We ate. We changed. I could read then.
Now Gram is dead, 'n' Mom, 'n' all but me.

'N' I'm near gone. M' mouth still squeaks
a sound 'r two. I *see*. I smell.
But no touch. 'S hard. 'N' hurts.
But them strawberries...they was big last spring. 'N'
sweet.

Insomnia

3 a.m. I'm wombly curled
Against my wife's warm side,
Beneath her arm.

Red-glow numerals flicker slowly—
3:01, :02, :03, :04—
God, at this pace morning pants a year away.

Legs burn. Muscles twitch movelessly
But twitch nonetheless, like a dying hound's
Dream-twitching, recalling distantly the pup.

:05, :06, :07—slower now. Slower
Than heartbeat, slower
Than sleep.

The red-glow numbers mid-flick freeze—
Sleep-breath beside me murmurs stasis.
Even breeze and stars stand silently still.

:08, :09—slower yet—heart-flesh flutters,
Eyelids droop finally—and I do not know
When I drift to death.

The Ripper's Daymare

Dank blood swirls there again, whorling darkly
In nubs of fingernails, splashed in worn-away
Spatters on pale calloused palms. Sleep
Is murdered now, acid-pungent sleep
Where *my* hot blood roils in peace.
Sleep dies—and red-rimed eyes
Confront the light, the blood
Benighted memories
Of shrieks and cries,
Screams of pain,
Knife-blood release,
Steaming gouts
Of dankly
Crimson
Blood

Part Three:
Songs of Mutabilitie

Fields of Starflowers

Fields of starflowers glitter
                            glitter
glisten as the hydrodrive
descends.
They glitter, glisten,
slide to shattered dissolution in flame
and ash—
a thousand generations lòst
in one flash-flare
of ion-blue.

The fields of starflowers waver
                             waver
Quaver in their common cry
as death approaches.
And metal soles disturb the ash
still smouldering and hot—
all that remains of a planet's soul.

The fields of starflowers haunting
                              haunting—
quantum memories
of whàt the New Ones
will never understand.

When the Wordmonger Came

When the wordmonger came
and spread his wares beneath
our alien shade
we wandered one by one
toward his ship
to touch our tongues
on new, exotic shapes.
We fondled and we fell in love,
we started back in shock,
we grew and changed.

And when he packed and left,
spinning out to planets
far from ours,
we shared our purchases,
cultivated them
watched them grow.
And after many days
the newness atrophied.
The words no longer touched
as much,
as deeply....
But we were different
and we knew it would happen once again
when the wordmonger returned.

Star Poet's Curse

I ask for images,
invoke whatever muses
there still may be...
and Galaxies explode
swirl
collide
and coalesce,
collapsing into uni-
verses—
sight and sound and
touch

In that kaleidoscopic
chaos
lie the bones
of infinities.
I must choose
which and how
to weld in line and
sound
and rhythm *thrumming*
with the life of finite
worlds.

And while I write
I despair—
in that always of possi-
bilities
how...how can I give
true life
to that one world
that changes all I know
and am.

I, Witness

for Bruce Boston

from Point Dume
you can see the arc
of Santa Monica Bay
bow-taut
bent like a scimitar—

at the distant point
a Devil Tree
blossoms death—

and waves of heat
and blindness
caress the coast

vaporizing Malibu

and where I stand
on Point Dume

On Reading the Stories of Orson Scott Card

I

Invisible man
launches himself in null-g—
Sacrificial Lamb

II

His sacrifice cut deeply—
Sliced flesh to flesh,
Harvested flesh from flesh.

Deeply unwept tears
Bore acid furrows in a soul
Roiled with lost souls.

They shed tears of pain and fear,
And cursed his steps,
Spat their blood beneath his steps.

Fear and hate and love
Compounded in his act—

And love defined the sacrifice:
Their pain for life—
His pain for greater, deeper life.

III

Music. It cuts, it severs heart
        from mind and hand
    and in their place, a residue,
        a glory, and a song.

IV

On a distant world (*almost*
Beyond the Eye of God)
A sparrow falls with none to mourn
And none to see.
On that world he kneels, stigmata palms
Resting on bent knees,
Kneeling beneath a darkness
Rood-shadow thin.

And weeps.
The knife glints—his feet twist
Beneath his weight
And ghost their pain along his arms.

His temples throb.
His side pours agony
Like heated wine.
And yet....

And yet the point drops
Pierces
Penetrates
And spills new blood upon *this* earth.

On a distant world, *(obscured almost*
From God's full Love)
A knife descends. A Christ
Completes his deadly sacrifice.

V

Is it enough to think the pain?
Speak the Sacrifice?

Does it benefit the more to *feel* the slice
of Shepherd's blade?
The nothingness of severed hands
Beneath the urgency of music never born?

Should I link to suffering
And share it through the mind?
Or be—just *be*—a pain-drawn Christ
Kneeling beneath the Tree of Sacrifice

The SoulOrgan

As they settle back, my congregation
rests heavy heads on plastic terminals
and plug themselves in, soul by soul.

I play. I pry their willing separation
from crude consciousness. My digitals
read out a crimson sentience-glow.

I couple rank to rank. An integration,
cybernetic blend of steel and mental
force, begins its cleansing, flexing flow.

I thumb a stop—and threaten shrill damnation
screaming in empty eyes, until integral
shunts close their silent howls....

And then I play salvation to sick souls,
gently disconnect the console terminals,
and watch the mundane drown my congregation.

The Star-Scout Handbook

They still call it summer camp
On this world
Without seasons.

Our tents are plastic bubble-domes
Conserving moisture and body heat
Against the vacuum.

Laser-blades hang dumbly
From synthetic belts as if in fact
Archaic pocket knives.

At night, close-wrapped
In mono-filaments,
We watch distorted star shapes

Flicker like lost memories.
We drouse. We sleep.
And dream the sterile dreams of haunted Earth.

Bodies

Weight—
heavy weighting down
of airier stuff
in birth

At first lifting a hand, leg
head
strains spirit

and parents boast
when baby turns, sits,
and stands

proof that matter has now grown
beyond the spirit's
weightlessness

Weight—
heavier weighing down
of life:

muscles, tissue,
calcium,
age, disuse, disease

lumps of cancer
blacken lungs
squeeze air
and breath

and death—that touch
which separates
weight from waitlessness

and spirit soars again
purified
and rises to the skies
in light

Our Gods Have Died

Our gods have died—
upon a cross,
upon a pyramid of bloodied stone

or in a test-tube,
a red-stained slide
bright in a microscope's false glare.

They died in launches
bursting barriers
and opening Systems to our touch.

They died in photographs
of frozen moons
scarred with ash though centuries from fires.

They died and died
and died again—

and yet

in sunset glows across
the pinnacles,
in glints of gold they breathe—

they breathe and pulse
and flow below
blood rhythms and breath stress—

in the atoms, molecules
of flesh and blood
beat the living gods of old.

Star-Pilot's Funeral
For My Father

I was six years out when the holo' came.
Six years...but for me two
brief days. I heard the buzz of a wasp's
harsh moan. I saw the stud

that, glowing, warned me that the ones
behind had something they
believed could be of interest
to an Earth-lost soul like me.

I touched the glow. It felt cool, dry.
I heard the static grow.
I swiveled in my module seat
to face the holo' screen.

He lay there, dressed in white like some
archaic bride-to-be.
He lay there, eyes pinched gently closed,
his lips like two thin bands

where once full smiles bloomed. He lay
unmoving, not a breath
disturbed the satin of his tie.
He lay...my father. Dead

I stared as minute-months sped by,
and dared not move, dared not
so much as lift my gaze from him.
Occasionally a hand

stretched out to touch a sunken cheek,
to touch a wrinkled brow,
or smooth a grey-strand hair above
his ear. I dared not move.

The static cracked. The stud-glow died.
The holo' disappeared.
My father disappeared. Oh, it
was possible to call

the image from computer files
and reassert his death
upon the holo'-screen. I
could watch as often as

I wished as days stretched into years,
years into centuries.
Already his soft dust had mixed
with Earth-soil on the world

that he had treasured...that I had left
behind for all. He
was gone. His bones would twist and crumble
in the space of time

it took for me to draw a breath
and touch a fingertip
to moisture I had not believed
to feel. And in the time

I have been sitting here—him dead,
gone beyond my touch—
I have sped centuries away,
drawn inches nearer to
the center of our Galaxy

Incubus

She watched the night-news re-cap at eleven
On the last gasp of cable from LA, then let the channel

Fade to starstorm flurries of angry static.
The video place had upped its price that day—

Five-fifty for a first-run film,
And she was too incensed by the blatant rip-off

(It was the only rental outlet in this burg)
To waste her money there.

·So she sat and smoked and drank and stared
At nothingness enfleshed in patterns on the

Dark oak paneling of the rented room.
The static grew insistently.

She stretched, she let her nubbly robe
Drift open and the snow of breasts

And waist and thighs
Matched the flurries on the set

That coalesced, extruded, blended
With the dark oak paneling

And he stood naked by her knees
As she leaned back and smoked and stared

At watermarks that marred the hypnotic
Cartography of cheap ceiling tiles.

Once she moaned and bit her lip.
Once she cried.

At dawn she woke. Exhausted. Sore.
Bloody. Depleted fullness and
Dampened fears. The channel flickered through
Its test pattern, giving birth to some

Charlatan selling ginsu knives or cars,
She did not know or care which one.

Succubi

When shadows fall and echoes call
Like ravens, tree to tree;
When living light grows black with blight—
They come to ravage me.

My chamber chills, the silence builds
And pulses in my ear.
They are not far—my door's ajar—
My body groans pale fears.

I will them gone, yet wait alone,
My blood a fevered heat.
They come...they smile...and without guile
They nestle at my feet.

A hand rests high upon my thigh
And burns with frightening cold—
And yet I know its icy glow
Obscures a steely hold.

How light, how deft—and I am left
A hostage to her charms;
And lip to lip I gladly slip
To hell within her arms.

Another runs ecstatic thumbs
Along my ribs and spine.
My life-blood thrills with savage chills;
I turn to make her mine...

And see the lies of empty eyes,
Of carmine lips like blood—
Deep inside, where saneness hides,
I freeze in numbing flood.

I try to scream as now the dream
Of love illicit dies;
Flesh bleeds the tone of fleshless bone
And sockets without eyes.

Yet teeth they have—in blackened caves
Of lust and passions bound;
They rend my skin, they pierce within,
Their bones illusion-gowned.

For still I see upon my knee
A form in beauty wrapped;
But as I stare, with hideous glare
The flesh with rot grows gapped.

Where once raged lust now burns dead dust,
I scream, I cry, I burst.
Where manblood flows their substance glows
To beauty, as at first.

At dawn my scars will fade like stars
That glimmer, gasp, and die;
In dawn's dim glow, I'll know—*I'll know*—
The treachery of their lie.

For though I've felt their passions' welts,
My body's lethal bane,
Grey twilight's breath shall twine with death
And pass my door again.

Gargoyles

Grant the fact I've had a nip or two—
Alcohol may be best at times like this,
Riding subways through living shadows,
Glints of shadoweyes
Orange-red between the stations,
Yellow eyes that move with mine.
Laugh if you wish! But next time glance up,
Examine black cathedral cornices where yesterday
Silent gargoyles crouched.

Faces of Fear
For Dean R. Koontz

Starblood mars a harvest moon—
Night chills rustle burgeoning cat-tails as
Twilight eyes glint through icy, thirst-slaked dark now
Shattered by an endless echoing moan.
Phantoms? the man devoutly hopes, though he knows
Watchers are abroad this night.
                         Ragged, raging
Lightning slices darkness to reveal a form,
Dragonfly perhaps, but monstrous, huge, a vapid
Mask bestowing nightmare anonymity on fact—
Beastchild hovering, preying for the
Strangers who must come (*the long-awaited*
Invasion of the errant wolfish humankind who fear
the
Shadowfires of the dawn) and give it leave to feed.

Malibu and Thousand Oaks, California
September, 1989